Bigfoot Sasquatch Files

Volume 3

By Kevin E. Lake

These stories are true.

Potentially...

Footprints In The Sand...

Big Ones!

It was so much easier to be an atheist back in college, Jason thought, barrelling down the road, en route to another Bigfoot

Sasquatch organization gathering. This weekend's trip was taking him to Corolla, a small, desolate village on the northern tip of the Outer Banks of North Carolina. At least he'd get some sun and sand, he thought, as he crossed the long bridge over the sound at Point Harbor. Take a nice little beach break after bursting some hillbilly belief bubbles, he thought, chuckling to himself as he made sure not to go more than five miles over the speed limit. He *did* have out-of-state plates, afterall.

What in the hell did Bigfoot Sasquatch have to do with being an atheist?

Simple.

The belief in Bigfoot Sasquatch, or other cryptids, was pretty much one of the few belief systems left that one could still publicly denounce, and who's believers one could still ridicule and shame for possessing a belief in things unseen- the very definition of faith- and *not* get locked up under the jail house for so doing. Or, in Jason's case, have their hand over fist money making social media accounts demonetized. All other belief systems based on faith were off limits.

Jason had missed the turbulent sixties, not having been born until the seventies, but he was happy to come of age during the nineties when there was a resurgence in bashing all things traditional, short lived as it was. And at first, as a caucasion male of European descent, he'd struggled with the concept of viewing himself as the root cause of all things bad in the world, but hey, he figured if he could hate so many people he didn't know personally, like all those Bible beating Christians, he could learn to hate himself to some degree, at least.

It took time, but he knew he'd achieved his goal of internalizing at least a small percentage of self hatred when he caught himself crying at the sight of his pasty pale skin in the mirror one morning. That was the morning when he had to have a heart to heart with himself about never having asked to be born white. But since he had been, and since he recognized that it was due to no choice of his, he could now relate even more to others who he felt were victims of circumstance, because now, he was one of them. He'd made the transition! He was practically a self made martyr! And man, did he feel guilty about it.

Jason had lost hope when that Texan took over the White House, the one whose father had stunk the place up during most of Jason's childhood, either as the man in charge, or as the man in charge's right hand man before that, when that no good actor from California was stinking the place up. Just as Jason was really beginning to enjoy his love hate relationship with himself, and participating in protests almost every week, he feared the geo-political winds were beginning to blow him in the direction of growing up and getting over himself, and his causes, for good.

Jason was all but ready to pack it in when the twin towers fell, because they'd fallen by the hands of followers of the wrong faith. How was he supposed to make Christians look like the most vile sect of believers in the history of God's green earth after this?

But then Jason discovered the train promoting the idea that not all Muslims were terrorists and not all terrorists were Muslims, which he and most level headed people knew to be true. But Jason, rarely level headed in regard to his hatred of all things traditional, quickly found the specific car on this train where all aboard went the extra mile of demonizing Christians and Christianity, by claiming all Christians were singling out all Muslims in the aftermath of the attacks. He jumped on board with his fellow radical leftists who saw the opportunity of a new way of going out and actively bashing the members of the Christian faith, and alas, he felt as if he'd refound his place in life.

And then the millennials came of age- those twerpy little snot nosed rugrats his sister used to babysit- and it wasn't okay to hate or bash *anyone*. Being nice was king, and since Jason was nearing fifty, he feared that being nice was here to stay, at least while he was still around, so he had to figure out another way.

And that's when he discovered Bigfoot Sasquatch!

Rather, those who believed in him, her, it or they.

"This is perfect!" Jason screamed, jumping up from his desk chair when the idea hit him several years before. "These people are idiots! And most of them are rural, backwood, family oriented Christians! I can bash these idiots all day long for believing in a bunch of ignorant horseshit no one's ever seen, just like God and Jesus, and I can get away with it and still make bank on social media doing it! This is *not* a protected group!"

Jason had spent most of his years after college as a newspaper writer, but like most of those guys lucky enough to still be relatively young when social media came out, he discovered that he could make way more money by blogging. He'd developed halfway decent writing skills through the years, and what he lacked in ability he made up for with passion. He poured his heart and soul into writing about what he loved.

Hate.

Namely, hating Christians and anything remotely conservative or traditional.

He'd developed quite the following through the years, and with each passing change in what would and would not be tolerated as far as hate in American society went, they were happy to jump ship with him when he had to leave one social media platform (that whole demonetization thing) and join another.

He'd been stuck at a pass when he got the idea to go about bashing Bigfoot Sasquatch believers. He'd been making bank blogging and posting his blogs on Facebook. That leftist leaning Mark Zuckerberg had no problem with him pointing out how ignorant Christians were, as long as they were American Christians. Jason laughed for years, when his competitors would post a meme to their Facebook pages referring to Islam as a religion of hate, and then end up having their accounts suspended or removed, knowing he could bash Christianity, labelling it as a religion of hate, or of incest and ignorance, or anything else bad he could think of, as much as he wanted on Facebook and get away with it, and he did.

But things changed after Zuckerberg started getting called out for his double standards by the rest of Silicon Valley and his advertisers. There had long stood an unspoken agreement between the billionaire entrepreneurs of the internet and the tax and regulate the hell out of everything Government men, and that unspoken agreement basically was that if the tech guys would mind their P's and Q's, then the Government men would take a laissez faire approach to the internet world (and of course there would be plenty of yacht parties with booze and drugs and 'she said she was legal' hookers for those Government men, courtesy of those Silicon Valley guys' lobbyists).

But Zuckerberg started bringing in the regulators with his shenanigans, like selling everyone's info to Chinese firms, so 'Ol Zuck started putting an end to the double standard bullcrap in a desperate attempt to make himself look good in the eyes of the people he'd conned, and thus, Jason found himself going from making tens of thousands of dollars a month bashing Christians and conservatives on Facebook to making zero dollars, and being banned, permanently, from the platform.

Enter YouTube, and Jason's ingenious idea of making a channel based on debunking these Bigfoot Sasquatch idiots. Oh, and how his somewhat massive following he'd collected through the years *loved* the idea as well, because they knew that most of the people who believed in such things were the very people they loved to hate as well.

Bigfoot!

Rubbish!

Just like God, and Jesus!

"Here we are," Jason said into his smartphone camera, "pulling up to the retreat." He was recording bits and pieces of his trip as he went along. He'd put it all together and upload and publish the video at the end of the weekend, and as most of his videos did, Jason was sure it would go viral.

***

Jason made sure to hang out in his car until a few minutes before the morning's first meeting started and then go into the rec center where the meetings for the weekend's festivities were being held. Actual Bigfoot Sasquatch hunts would take place later, on the beaches, and in the scrub brush, with several meetings, like the one Jason was about to enter, interspersed in between.

Jason had mastered his methods over the past couple of years, and today, he would do as he always did. He would sit during the meetings, act as if he was as interested, and like he believed in Bigfoot Sasquatch as much as everyone else in attendance, and then he would work his magic later by way of editing.

Jason entered the meeting and sat in the middle of the crowd, beside a couple in their late fifties. Jason knew that sitting in front might draw attention, and sitting in the back might make him look conspicuous, so sitting in the middle was the best way, as he saw it, to remain practically invisible.

"I'm so excited," Jason said, leaning over and speaking into the ear of the man beside him.

"Us, too," said the man's wife, leaning around her husband to do so, so that she could make eye contact with Jason as she spoke to him.

"First time?" Jason asked her.

"Oh, no," her husband said, answering for her. "We come to this one every year, and we usually make a couple of these a year. We were up at one in Virginia last month. The one where Dr. Drake spoke."

"Oh," Jason said, sounding excited. He knew of Drake and his work, as he was constantly attempting to debunk Drake's YouTube channel on his own. Unfortunately, he hadn't quite cracked the code for debunking Drake yet, because the man never actually claimed to see Bigfoot Sasquatch. He merely claimed to have potentially seen Bigfoot Sasquatch, and it's his channel's *viewers* who claim to see the alleged beast in the background of most of his videos. Boy, did Jason hate this Drake guy, and man, was he determined to get him someday, that bastard, Jason thought.

"That's awesome," Jason said. "I love Dr. Drake and his work."

"He's the best," the man's wife said.

"You know," Jason said, "I've been thinking about doing some stuff on social media myself, and I'd love to interview you guys a bit during this weekend's retreat, if it's okay with you."

"Why, sure," the couple said in unison. They had no idea they were dealing, not with the devil, but a man with devilish intent.

Jason had mastered his style of deception. He had learned to interview folks at Bigfoot Sasquatch retreats, just like this one, and then later think of different questions to edit into the video, so it appeared as if the people interviewed were actually answering questions they were never asked, but only Jason knew this. Jason was able to make them look completely ignorant and beyond ridiculous, and his hundreds of thousands of jaded viewers loved every minute of it, though they didn't realize they were being duped themselves by way of Jason's editing efforts. But they wouldn't have minded if they'd known, Jason knew, because, like him, they wouldn't care about the actual facts. Their minds were already made up.

***

With the first meeting of the day out of the way, the group of roughly thirty people in attendance for this weekend's Bigfoot Sasquatch retreat made their way out of the rec center and into the backs of pickup trucks that had football stadium bleachers built into them in order to seat as many people as possible. The trucks headed up the beach and into the brush, where very few people lived, where there were no paved roads, and where no one was allowed to feed the horses.

You see, in Corolla, there is a herd of wild Spanish ponies, and they're protected by the game and wildlife organizations of North Carolina, as well as a couple of various not for profit groups who make a *killing* on merchandise. The Bigfoot Sasquatch group guides talked about the importance of allowing the horses to remain wild, and ended by saying, "so if you see a Bigfoot Sasquatch, and you want to pet or feed him, her, it or they, that's fine. Do so at your own risk. But do not interfere, in any way, with the ponies!"

Bigfoot Sasquatch, ponies, whatever, Jason was thinking to himself, while eyeballing a cute girl in her mid twenties that he was *certainly* going to interview once the group got out of the trucks.

"Here we are," one of the guides said when the trucks stopped. "Again, break up into groups of three to five, spread out and see what you can see. Listen and see what you can hear. Remember to follow your nose, as well, as sometimes folks have reported to have smelled him, her, it or they. And let's all meet back in an hour for lunch. We'll eat, compare notes, then do another search before heading back and listening to one of our guest speakers lecture on the topic of which wild edibles are best to plant on your property in the hopes of attracting Bigfoot Sasquatch."

"Mind if I join you guys?" Jason said, jogging to catch up to the couple in their fifties he'd been talking to during the meeting. As luck would have it, the twenty something he'd been checking out in the truck was with them.

"Not at all," the girl said, turning at the sound of his voice, and smiling upon making eye contact. "My name is Becca."

"High, Becca," Jason said, extending his hand for a shake. "I'm Jason."

The groups all split up and went in separate directions. As some of the groups headed into the thick, bush scrub country that would pass for woods on the outer banks, Jason and his group remained on the beach, walking north, toward the Virginia state line.

"So how long have you been doing this?" Jason asked Becca, wondering if she'd smiled so nicely because she saw him more as the boy next door type he tried to portray, or if it was because she viewed him as one of her dad's friends types, which he'd always hated.

"First time," she said.

"Really," Jason said, surprised. "What inspired you to come?"

"My friend," she said. "Ricky."

"Who's Ricky?" Jason asked, hoping that he wasn't a boyfriend. "And what's his story?"

"Oh," he was just a friend from school," Becca said. "We'd been friends since we were kids."

Jason could tell that Becca was talking in past tense, and all of a sudden, he wasn't thinking about getting in her pants as much as he was interested in hearing about what happened to Ricky.

"What happened?" he asked.

"He died," Becca said. "About a year ago. A very rare cancer."

"Sorry to hear that," Jason said.

After walking further up the beach in silence for a full minute, Becca said, "he loved this Bigfoot Sasquatch stuff. We were actually going to come on this retreat together, but the angels swept him away before we could."

"Now, Becca," Jason caught himself saying before he could think before speaking, something he rarely did. "You don't really believe in that angel crap, do you?"

"Of course," Becca said. "Don't you?"

"Look!" It was the woman in her fifties. She and her husband were standing, frozen. "Something big and dark went behind that pile of brush over there!" She extended her right arm, her right index finger extended, pointing to the pile of brush.

"Come on," Jason said, taking Becca by the hand and beginning to run with her, toward the brush pile, seeing the opportunity to take his foot out of his mouth. "Let's check it out."

Jason and Becca and the married couple in their fifties grouped up behind a log about fifty yards behind the brush pile in question. "We'll go around on the left," the husband of the woman who'd potentially spotted the beast said. "You two go around the right!"

"Okay," Jason said. He took Becca by the hand and began to lead her in the direction in which they'd been assigned to go. She all too willingly followed, which led Jason to believe she'd forgiven him his trespasses, as these Christian types would say, and some actually had a tendency to do so, though those were not the ones Jason liked to focus on.

As the married couple made their way around the far side of the brush pile, and out of sight of Jason and Becca, Jason and Becca made their way around the other side, where they soon discovered the large, dark object that the woman had apparently seen.

"Jesus Christ!" Jason said, staring at the black Spanish pony. "A fucking horse!"

"Wow," Becca said. "Is that language really necessary? And, do you really need to take the Lord's name in vain?"

"The Lord," Jason said. "What Lord?" He walked over to Becca, until the distance between them couldn't have been more than a foot. "There is no Lord," Jason said. "There is no God. And there certainly is no such thing as Bigfoot Sasquatch!"

And that's when the Spanish pony, which Jason had gotten too close to while closing his distance with Becca, came up behind him and kicked him in the back of the head and knocked him the fuck out!

***

"Your parents were fucking deranged."

Jason heard the voice, but he hadn't seen who it belonged to. His eyes were closed. His head was throbbing, and he tasted blood. "What?" he said.

"I said your parents were fucking deranged."

Jason sat up, and sitting beside him, in the sand, was a man about his age, wearing a tie dyed t-shirt with a peace sign on the front. The man didn't have long hair, and he didn't have a beard, but it looked like he could use a haircut and a shave. Five o'clock shadow stuff. Too busy this week to make it to the barber.

"But don't worry," the man said. "We've reserved a special place in hell for them, and, well, they've taken up their reservations."

"Who the hell are you?" Jason said, trying to rise to his feet and falling back on his ass.

"Don't try to move," the man said. "You pissed that horse off pretty bad. Didn't they tell you on the way up that the horses don't like loud noises?"

Jason passed out, only momentarily, and when he woke up, he found that the man who'd been speaking was now carrying him down the beach.

"I'm sorry you endured all the abuse," the man carrying him said, when he saw that Jason's eyes were open. "Having to put up with all that bullshit. Always being told you were not good enough. Unworthy. And the beatings. No child deserves that."

"Then why the fuck did it happen?" Jason asked. It was the same question he'd asked countless therapists and thousands upon thousands of bottles of beer.

"That, my friend," the man said, "is a question that only my boss can answer. It's far above my paygrade."

And Jason passed out again.

"...you're going to get nothing but disappointment," the man said as Jason came to again.

"What?" Jason said.

"I said that if you hold everyone of a certain belief to such bullshit standards because your parents were fucked up, you're going to get nothing but disappointment. There are many wonderful Christians, Jews, Muslims and Budhists in this world. There are plenty of wonderful atheists whose seats are already reserved in Heaven."

Jason wanted to say *what?*, but he passed out again before he could.

When Jason awoke again, he was no longer being carried, but he was not alone, either. All roughly thirty members of the Bigfoot Sasquatch weekend retreat were there, in front of him, looking up the beach, in awe, as he came to.

Jason turned to look in the direction in which they were staring. For just an instant, he could have sworn that he saw a large, dark figure, a couple of hundred yards up the beach, duck into a stand of trees at the edge of the forest.

Jason's eyes worked their way back from the point where he believed he'd seen the dark figure, all the way back to where he sat, and what he saw was a single pair of footprints in the sand.

Big ones.

The End

Swimfan

(Originally Titled: "I Saw A Bigfoot Sasquatch And It Ruined My Life!")

"You're on the air. Go!"

"So, like. Am I on the air now? Live? Or is this being pre-recorded to be played later?"

"You're on the air, live. Now. Go."

Nick hated his job, and he didn't even need the money. But he had to work, per the judge's order. Nick was on probation for a year for his first D.U.I. conviction. He hoped it would be his last, but who knew. The whole twelve step program thing wasn't really working for him because, admittedly, he wasn't working it. That, too, had all been judge ordered.

"So like, I know Bigfoot Sasquatch is real, because he tried to rape my girlfriend back in college."

"Go on," Nick said to the caller, sounding interested, but totally rolling his eyeballs in the privacy of his a.m. radio station's small boothe. The radio station's office was in a spare room above a shity little regional bank. It was triangular shaped, due to the building's design, but it worked. Just enough space to serve the station's twenty thousand weekly listeners and growing (hopefully).

"I swear to God, it wasn't me! I'll tell ya that!" the caller said. "I didn't touch that bitch, and she was just trying to ruin my life, and that's exactly what she did. And it was that goddamn Bigfoot Sasquatch's fault for helping her!"

"Next caller," Nick said, hanging up on yet another psychopath, as he saw it. "And please, folks, let me remind you to watch your language when we're live. My grandmother's listening."

It wasn't true. Nick's grandmother had died when he was a very young child. But Nick was good at lying. All part of the job.

And it wasn't the belief in Bigfoot Sasquatch that he was lying about. He never claimed to believe or disbelieve. He figured anything was possible. The dishonest part came in pretending to give a shit about what the people who called into the show, his show, were calling about.

When Nick's very rich parents found out their very rich son was being ordered to work, they called Nick's very rich uncle who owned a radio station and hit him up for a favor. Nick's very rich uncle jumped at the opportunity to help his favorite nephew, little Nicky, because he agreed with Nick's parents, that Nick would absolutely *not* get some kind of labor job. Nick, despite being born into privilege, never took advantage of his circumstances and went to college or picked up any specific skill sets, because, he figured, what was the use? His grandmother who had died when he was a young child had invented waterproof cameras (she'd been an avid photographer and scuba diver), so it was highly unlikely anyone in the family would ever have to work for many, many, many generations.

Unless they were dumb enough to go out and get a D.U.I.

So here Nick was now, hosting the Bigfoot Sasquatch hour for his very rich uncle, in this little studio, putting up with total weirdos, as he saw it, but at least keeping his probation officer off his back in doing so.

"Am I on the air?" the caller said.

"You are," Nick said. "Go."

"Is this Nick?"

"The one and only," Nick said, rolling his eyes, but not as outrageously as he had toward the rapist.

"I know what you're doing," the caller said. "And I don't like it."

"Oh?" Nick said, hoping not everyone in the whole damn listening area knew about his D.U.I. Not that he cared, but still. "So what is it that I'm doing?"

"You're making fun of those of us who believe in Bigfoot Sasquatch."

"I've never done that," Nick said, surprised at hearing the defensiveness in his voice. "That's not who I am." And he was actually being honest about that. He never got his jollies off by making fun of anyone for any reason. He just liked to drink beer and watch sports.

"You're trying to pit believers and non-believers off against each other so you can sit back and laugh as we argue."

"Who is this?" Nick said.

"It's none of your goddamn business who this is," the caller said, just before Nick hung up on him due to his language.

"Okay," Nick said. "If you guys don't cut it with the language, I'm going to have to play some previously recorded phone calls. And that's no fun. So please watch your mouths. Remember. My grandmother."

Nick got lucky. No one else cussed for the rest of his shift, and he was able to kill the time in a much more relaxed way. An "uh huh" here and an "uh huh" there- here an "uh huh," there an "uh huh" and his shift was over.

"How in the name of God can you listen to those idiots without laughing your ass off?" Nick's best good beer drinking buddy, Quinn said, as Nick got into the passenger side of Quinn's car. Quinn was really good about taking Nick to work and picking him up and taking him back home afterward. Nick had also lost his license for a year due to the D.U.I. It helped that Nick was paying Quinn for it. A hundred dollars a day. Plus all the free beer the two of them could drink together, which was a lot. Nick knew he could possibly be given a piss test at any time, and if he popped hot, he would have to serve the rest of his time in jail. He had three months to go, and he figured he'd rather be in jail than stay sober. What was the difference, was how he saw it.

"My uncle would fire me," Nick said, reaching into the cooler between his feet, and then opening up the can of Devil's Backbone Vienna Lager he'd pulled out of it. None of that Bud

Light shit for Nick. That was for rednecks and hillbillies. "Besides," he said after taking a long swig. "I've heard it all."

"That last guy," Quinn said, pointing to the radio, and then shutting it off. "A fucking Bigfoot Sasquatch kept him from being able to sell his house? Because everyone knew there was a Bigfoot Sasquatch in the area? So he got foreclosed on, and his finances have been shit ever since? He tried to make it sound like Bigfoot Sasquatch ruined his life."

"I get so much of that Bigfoot Sasquatch ruined my life shit," Nick said, and then he took another drink. "It's all the same. People claim to have seen Bigfoot Sasquatch, then they tell people about it, then they're written off as crazy, and they have no friends, and their wives leave them. They try to make it sound like seeing a Bigfoot Sasquatch is as shell shocking as going off and fighting in a goddamn war or something."

"Oh," Quinn said, reaching into his front pants pocket as he made the turn onto Willow Road, which would take them to Nick's house. Rather, Nick's parents' grand estate, on the back part of which had been built Nick's house ten years before when he'd hit the age of majority. He still spent quite a bit of time at mommy and daddy's though. Especially around meal time. "Some guy said to give you this."

"What's this?" Nick said, taking the folded piece of paper Quinn had handed him. He opened in up and read the handwritten note aloud. "I know what you're up to."

Nick only had to think for a millisecond before remembering the caller he'd spoken to earlier who had accused him of making fun of people who believed in Bigfoot Sasquatch.

"Who the hell gave you this?" Nick said, turning his head to face Quinn.

"Some dude," Quinn said. "About ten minutes before you came out."

"What did he look like?" Nick asked. "Did he tell you his name?"

"No name," Quinn said. "He looked about our age. White guy. I'm not gay, but I'd say he was good looking."

"And he didn't tell you his name?" Nick said.

"That's pretty much what no name means, Nick."

Nick's family's estate was around the next turn. The two men finished up the short remainder of the trip in silence. Once there, they went into Nick's house (he referred to it as a cottage, as his parents did, even though it was five thousand square feet), and got shitty drunk while watching some sports team score more points than their opponent in some game.

***

"You're on the air," Nick said, nursing a hangover by drinking a Bloody Mary. Sure, it was night already, but Nick and Quinn had stayed up until the sun had come up drinking, so time, for Nick and the lifestyle he led, and Quinn as well, since becoming Nick's best friend shortly after moving to the area a year ago, was irrelevant. "Go."

"There is a freaking Bigfoot Sasquatch right outside my house right now," the caller said. Nick could hear the fear in the man's voice, and he often wondered how these Bigfoot Sasquatch people could be so convincing. Were they having some sort of psychotic episode when they supposedly saw these eight feet tall, eight hundred pound creatures? Nick was convinced that had to be it. Either psychotic episodes, or they were on drugs. Nick sure did like his weed, but he couldn't remember ever seeing Bigfoot Sasquatch after smoking up a big fat bowl.

"What is the Bigfoot Sasquatch doing?" Nick asked, trying to keep the caller on the line. One hour was a long time to fill, and Nick had found that the key to burning it up the best was by keeping callers who were willing to talk, and who didn't use profanity when they did, on the line for as long as possible.

"It's ruining my life," the caller said. "Right now. As we speak."

"Can you please explain to our listeners how, specifically, the Bigfoot Sasquatch that's outside your house is ruining your life?" Nick said. He never got a straight answer on this one.

"Well," the caller said, sounding really nervous. "He cost me my job."

"How," Nick began, "did the Bigfoot Sasquatch outside your house cost you your job?"

"I haven't been able to go to work for a week, and my boss called me today and fired me for excessive absences. That's how."

"How is it that the Bigfoot Sasquatch kept you from going to work for a week?" Nick asked.

"Because he's right outside my house!" the caller screamed into the phone. "I can't go outside and get in my fucking car and go to fucking…"

"Next caller," Nick said, wishing he'd hung up just a little sooner. At least soon enough to have missed the second F bomb.

"I bet you thought that guy was a blast," an eerily familiar sounding voice said on the other line.

"Who is this?" Nick said.

"You know who I am," the caller said.

"Ah," Nick said, remembering where he'd heard the voice. "My mystery caller from last night. You're the guy who thinks I'm pranking everyone."

"That's right, buddy boy. And I know that you know that I know exactly where you are right now."

"You and our up to twenty thousand other listeners," Nick said, trying to sound brave, but feeling a little creeped out.

"You know what I think would be funny, Nick?" the caller said. "If you ran into one of these creatures one dark night, and he ripped your legs off and beat you over the head with them."

"That's not a very nice thing to say," Nick said.

"You have no idea what these people who've actually seen these things have gone through," the caller said. "Their lives have been absolutely destroyed, and then you sit up there in your little c budget radio station and make fun of us?"

"Wait a minute," NIck said. "I get it. You just said, *us*. So obviously, you've seen Bigfoot Sasquatch, too."

"Of course I have, you idiot!"

"Okay," Nick said. "How about instead of calling me and accusing me of doing something I'm not, like making fun of our loyal listeners, and insulting me, and wishing violence upon me, why don't you just tell us your story? Where and when did you see the Bigfoot Sasquatch? Under what circumstances? And most importantly, how in the name of God did it ruin your life?"

"Keep laughing," the caller said. "Bigfoot Sasquatch might not show up and give you the ass whooping you deserve, but by God, I will!"

And then the mysterious caller hung up.

"Just so you'll know, guys," Nick said, his voice riding over the sound of the dial tone from the disconnected call, "we have the ability to trace our calls. We can find you. It's not a good idea to call and make threats of violence with twenty thousand witnesses listening in. Keep that in mind as you're calling in. You don't want the boys in blue showing up at your house."

But that was all bullshit, and Nick was scared. He was texting away to Quinn as he was speaking the words over the radio.

"Don't worry," Quinn texted back, almost immediately. "I'm in the parking lot, and I heard the call. That crazy son of a whore will have a baseball bat waiting on him when he gets here if he's dumb enough to come."

Nick felt instantly relieved. He had no idea what forces in the cosmos were at work when Quinn had decided to uproot from his normal day job in Akron, Ohio (the type of job where they actually gave you five company polo shirts instead of three, so you wouldn't have to do laundry until the weekend if you didn't want to) a little more than a year ago, and move him into Nick's community. Further, he had no idea how the cosmos had arranged for Quinn to replace one of the guys on the lawn crew his family had used for years, shortly after Nick had gotten his D.U.I. and had started working at the radio station, but he was thankful it had happened.

And Nick was thankful for that first day that he'd met Quinn. The first day Nick had met Quinn, when he, Nick, had been binge drinking by the pool, and he'd asked Quinn if he wanted a beer, and Quinn said yes, and he did take a beer, and he did drink it, and he did not return to work with the rest of the crew, because he felt it was more important to drink a beer with the customers' adult son, and Nick knew he'd found a kindred soul. And when Quinn did get fired by the lawn crew boss for drinking with the customers' adult son instead of mowing grass, Nick did hire him to be his private driver.

Nick and Quinn had been inseparable, and rarely sober, since.

***

"So what in the hell do you think this guy's deal is?" Quinn asked Nick on the way home. Nick was already pounding down the brewskies.

"I have no fucking idea," Nick said.

The mysterious caller who'd alluded to hurting Nick had not shown up at the radio station, rather, the bank, with the radio station in the broom closet upstairs. Either that, or he had shown up, but when he'd seen Quinn's car, he decided not to stick around. This is what Quinn thought, at least, and he'd said as much to Nick.

"Why do you think that he thinks that you're making fun of people who claim to have seen Bigfoot Sasquatch?" Quinn asked.

"Gee, I don't know," Nick said. "Maybe becasue I fucking do?"

Quinn was silent for a moment. Confused. "Wait a minute," he said. "I thought you were, like, agnostic about the whole Bigfoot Sasquatch thing. That you didn't even care if he, she, it, or they exist or not?"

"I am," Nick said. "Shit, there might be some out there. I don't know, and I don't care." He popped the top of another beer, and then he said, "but how can you not make fun of the backwoods redneck fucks who claim to have actually seen one. They set themselves up. It's too fucking simple!"

Quinn continued to drive in silence. Nick paid no never mind, because he was too busy drinking beer and being thankful that Quinn had been on time, like he always was, and had saved him a potential ass beating.

When they got home, they went inside and watched some sports team score more points than their opponent, and got shitty drunk, and they did not go to bed until after the sun came up.

***

When Nick woke up late afternoon the next day, he found a note on the kitchen counter beside the coffee pot.

I made you breakfast. It's in a tupperware container in the ref. Just Nuke it. I'll be out running errands, and when I come home, I'll have more food. Don't worry. I'll be back in time to take you to work, boss.

Quinn

"A saint," Nick said to himself after reading Quinn's note. "The man is a fucking saint."

After a couple of cups of coffee, Nick nuked his breakfast and ate it, and then he made himself a Bloody Mary and went outside to sit under the shade of the giant magnolia tree his grandfather had planted a million years ago. God, he hated hangovers, but at least in three more months, when he got off probation, he'd be able to sleep them off entirely, like he always had in the past, because he wouldn't have to have his stupid job down at his uncle's stupid radio station anymore.

"How's that ex-con working out for you?"

The words rang in Nick's head like a gong. It was the voice of Chick, the head guy of the lawn crew.

"What?" Nick said, turning his head to his left to see Chick making his way over.

Chick pulled up a seat and stuffed the cold hard cash that Nick's parents had just given him for payment for last month's lawn care in his wallet. Chick wasn't an idiot. He knew these rich fuckers hated paying taxes as much as he, one of the truly hard working men of the world did, so he gave them two prices when they inquired about his services. There was the competitive, fair market value price which he'd offer to customers who paid with a check or credit card, and then there was the deeply discounted price he offered to anyone willing to pay him in cash. Chick made a lot of money and he didn't give much of it to the IRS because of his scheme, and his customers thought of him as a genius for doing it. They envied the way a man who actually had to work for his money could stick it to the IRS in such a slick way. It wasn't quite as easy for them to do it, with all their trust fund dividend and interest income being fully taxable, and all. They hated the IRS for taking so much of what they'd rightly been born into, so they loved the way Chick handled the bastards. He was their hero.

"That con you've got living with you," Chick said, sitting down and then adjusting his position in his chair, now that his wallet was so much fatter than it had been the last time he'd sat down anywhere. "Quinn."

"What do you mean, con?" Nick asked, and then he took a sip of his Bloody Mary.

"He didn't tell you?" Chick said. "As much time as you guys spend together?"

"Quinn's not a con," Nick said, surprised at the sound of his own voice. So defensive. It was as if someone had just told him his girlfriend was a slut. "He's a damned dependable dude. He always gets me to work on time, and he's never late in picking me up. And he runs all kinds of extra errands and stuff that he's not even paid to do."

"Whatever, chief," Chick said, rising to leave. "Just don't piss him off."

"Why?" Nick asked.

"He'll beat the living shit out of you like he did that poor bastard in Texas. Did three years for that one."

"Texas," Nick said, sounding incredulous. "He's never said shit about Texas. He's from Ohio."

Chick laughed so hard he nearly fell down. "That fucker's never been to Ohio," he said.

"Where did you hear all this?" Nick said.

"Dude," Chick said, walking back to get within feet of Nick before speaking again. "I hire my guys through the courts and probation officers. These are guys that can't get most jobs due to background checks. I knew this shit about Quinn before I even met him."

"You've got to be shitting me," Nick said, and all of a sudden, he found himself believing what he was being told.

"Look," Chick said, shrugging his shoulders. "People can change. Maybe he has. Just be careful."

And then Chick turned and walked away, heading off to collect his cash from the Browns down the road. He loved the Browns, because they, too, paid in cash, allowing him to stick it to the IRS, and the Browns loved Chick for doing it, because they couldn't, because the poor bastards had been born into extreme wealth and the IRS was all over them.

***

"Think you'll get any psycho calls tonight?" Quinn asked Nick several hours later on the way to work.

"I'm sure I'll get a few," Nick said. "It's the nature of the beast."

"Pun intended?" Quinn said, and they both laughed.

"As long as I don't get a call from one specific psycho," Nick said, and he slightly turned his head toward Quinn to see if he could note a reaction. "The night will go just fine."

"Oh," Quinn said after a moment's hesitation. "Don't worry about that guy. I'll wait outside in the parking lot your whole shift if it makes you feel safer."

"It's okay," NIck said. "That's a long time to sit in a parking lot. Just be on time. If he calls back and makes more threats, I'll call the damn police."

Quinn dropped Nick off at the bank and then drove off. Nick hurried up to the office and replaced Jillian, a very lovely woman in her sixties who hosted *The B Sides.* And no, it wasn't a radio show showcasing big bands' lesser known songs. It was literally a show about bees. Honey bees. Jillian was a hippy, and Nick's very rich uncle had the hots for her, so he gave her her own radio show where she could talk about bees. It hadn't paid off for Nick's very rich uncle, as when he pressed Jillian for something in exchange, he found out she had a girlfriend. And only five hundred weekly listeners tuned in for the show. But Nick's very rich uncle kept Jillian and her show, anyway, because he liked Jillian.

And he hoped some day he would be able to turn her.

"We have something extra special for our listeners tonight," Nick said into the mic as he started his show. "Throwback Thursday! Even though it's Tuesday! That's right. We are going to start the show off by playing some of our best calls from the past. Let's get started with that guy from Pennsylvania who woke up one morning to find a couple of Bigfoot Sasquatches in his recently drained swimming pool!"

As Nick's listeners were hearing the story told from the guy who called a couple of months back, claiming that he had a suspicion Bigfoot Sasquatch was swimming in his pool at night, so he'd drained his pool, and ended up catching two of the creatures when they'd jumped into an empty pool on the deep end and ended up breaking their legs and therefore couldn't get out, Nick began Googling the ever loving hell out of his best good friend Quinn. He didn't dare risk doing so at home earlier, out of fear that Chick was most certainly telling the truth and that Nick had a real psychopath on his hands in his good buddy Quinn, and that that real psychopathic friend of his might catch him Googling him and take offense to it.

"Shit!" Nick said, aloud, before even finding any hits online. He'd glanced over to the side of the desk and saw the note that someone had supposedly given Quinn to pass on to him in the parking lot from the other night. He still had Quinn's note from earlier in the day, the note about breakfast, in his pocket. He pulled it out and compared the two notes and he saw that the handwriting was identical. "Shit!" Nick said again, after making the realization, and just because he liked to say the word shit.

As the man from Pennsylvania was telling the listeners in his previously recorded audio that of course he didn't call the Government men about the Bigfoot Sasquatches in his pool, because he knew they'd disappear him if he did, Nick hit paydirt with his internet search. It turned out that Quinn was from Texas, and that he had served three years in prison for attempted manslaughter.

Quinn read several articles about the case, and as it turned out, Quinn had actually been sentenced to twenty five years. However, the man who he'd been convicted of beating almost to death, and having put into a comma, came out of that comma after Quinn had been in prison for three years and told his side of the story, and as it turned out...

...it was the exact same story Quinn had told!

During Quinns trial, he'd claimed that while his best friend Randy and himself were out camping at South Llano River Park, just outside of Junction, Texas, they'd been attacked and badly beaten by a Bigfoot Sasquatch. Quinn claimed he'd barely been able to make it out alive, and he feared that Randy was dead.

There were no witnesses to the incident, and when authorities arrived at the scene, they found Randy, beaten so badly that he was in a coma. There were thirty eight empty beer cans found at the campsite, and Quinn's blood alcohol content

(BAC) came back at more than three times the legal limit for driving after testing. Randy's BAC was about the same, but what had put him into the coma was blunt force trauma. Randy had been smacked in the head so hard that it knocked him out, and he stayed out, and on life support, for three years.

At the trial, Randy's family had gotten more than two dozen anti-character witnesses to claim that Quinn was pretty much the biggest piece of shit on earth. And the prosecutor claimed his whole story about Bigfoot Sasquatch was all being told in an attempt to claim insanity, because everyone knew there was no such thing as Bigfoot Sasquatch. In the end, the jury voted unanimously to convict him, and then the judge through the book at him.

However, when Randy finally woke from his coma, and was questioned by the authorities, he told the exact same story Quinn had told, and the Judge let Quinn out of prison early for good behavior. It was all done low key, so as not to draw media attention, but that one guy who has been kicked off of all the social media sites for blazing every conspiracy theory known to man, and who, ironically lives in Texas, got word of the release, and he went crazy with the story. That's how Nick had been able to find out all about it in the first place, here, tonight, while doing his Google searches.

"Oh, my God," Nick said aloud. "I get it. I get how having a Bigfoot Sasquatch encounter can ruin your life!"

Nick decided he would make things right, and he figured it might be a pretty good way of saving himself from an asswhooping that seemed to be coming his way pretty soon. When the guy from Pennsylvania, via replay, finished up about how all he could figure was that some other Bigfoot Sasquatches had come to the aid of the two he'd trapped in his pool the next night (because they were gone the next morning when he woke up, but by God, he swore, he was not lying), and the whole damn incident had ruined his life, Nick broke into the show to make a special announcement.

An apology.

"I have a very special statement I want to make tonight," Nick said, speaking into the mic. After a moment's pause, he said, "I'm sorry."

Nick let another moment pass before continuing, allowing his listeners' ears to prick up fully.

"I have never claimed to believe or disbelieve in the existence of Bigfoot Sasquatch," he said, being completely honest. "And I've always considered myself to be the kind of person who would never make fun of anyone else because of their beliefs. However, I've found myself doing that with many Bigfoot Sasquatch believers lately, and I humbly apologize. I would never make fun of someone for belonging to a specific religion, and I would certainly never make fun of someone due to their ethnicity or sexual preference. It's not okay to make fun of people who believe in Bigfoot Sasquatch, either."

Nick took a calculated pause before speaking again. He wanted to give what he'd just said time to sink in for his listeners, as well as see if he could get them to focus even more.

"I've only recently come to understand how having a run-in with one of these creatures could absolutely destroy one's life.

And I want to go further and say that if your life has been negatively affected due to your personal encounter with Bigfoot Sasquatch, I wish you nothing but healing. It is to you that I apologize the most, and it is from you, that I ask forgiveness."

Nick was finished. He'd said everything he could think of to say.

And the phones started ringing off the hooks!

Believers and non-believers alike were condoning Nick for taking the high road and doing the right thing. No one said anything mean about anyone else who might think differently than them (at least on *this* night), and Nick's mysterious caller, his swimfan, did not call at all.

When Nick's shift was over, like clockwork, Quinn was waiting on him in the parking lot. "Nice show," Quinn said as Nick got into the car and took a beer out of the cooler sitting on the floor of the passenger side. "Thanks," Nick said, as he cracked the can open. "And our mystery caller never called."

"He came by," Quinn said, handing Nick a piece of paper as he put the car in drive and began making his way out of the bank's parking lot.

Nick felt hesitant, but he wanted to get it over with, so he wasted no time in opening the note.

"You're forgiven," was all it said.

"Is this good news?" Nick asked Quinn, knowing the proof was always in the pudding, and in this instance, the tone of Quinn's voice would be the pudding.

"It's good," Quinn said. "I don't think you'll have any problems with that guy again.

The two of them went home and got blitzkrieg drunk while watching some sports team score more points than another in some sporting event, and they drank beer until the sun came up. Quinn continued driving for Nick until he got his license back, at which time he "went back to Ohio" for a job opportunity.

Nick hated to see Quinn go, but he was also relieved to a degree. He now felt like he could sleep with both eyes shut.

Unless, of course, he ever decided to go camping at South Llano River Park just outside Junction, Texas, in which case he knew it would be best to not sleep at all.

 On second thought, Nick thought, there are just some places he decided he'd never go, and South Llano River Park outside of Junction, Texas just became one of those places.

The End

3

Gaslighting

(Originally Titled: The Unfortunate Demise Of 'Crazy A')

Stacy Pierce sat on her front porch. *Her* being the keyword
here, because it was actually hers. No one else's. She wasn't
paying some landlord *her* money to sit on *his* front porch. She
was paying PennyMac to sit on *her* front porch.

Okay, so it was the bank's front porch, but the deed was in
Stacy Pierce's name, and that was what mattered, because
Stacy Pierce was a first time homebuyer, by God and Jesus
and all the saints and sinners, too!

Stacy sat on that front porch of her's (we'll ignore the whole
mortgaged for life thing for now), and she stared out into the
woods that made up her front yard and that lined her
driveway, and that went to the road, across which there were
more woods. She tried to remember a more triumphant time in
her life, and though there had been many triumphant times in
her life- graduating at the top of her class Yale School of Law,
etc.- none of them, at least that she could remember, felt so
satisfying as this moment right now.

"Hi," Stacy heard the woman's voice call. Stacy looked down
at the foot of the driveway, about one hundred yards down the
hill, and she saw a woman, appearing to be in her mid-fifties,
and very tall as far as American women in their mid fifties
went, standing there, waving.

"Hi," Stacy said, waving and standing simultaneously. The woman simply stood there, at the end of the driveway, saying no more, but continuing to wave and smile, eerily, Stacy thought, like the Joker from the Batman series. "Would you like to come up?" Stacy said, not knowing if she was doing the right thing or not, but the tall woman seemed harmless enough.

"My name is Stacy," Stacy said, extending her hand for a shake after the tall woman made it up the drive and to the bottom step of the porch where Stacy had gone to greet her. "I'm new here. Just moved in."

"I know," the tall lady said. "I saw the moving trucks, but I've just stopped today, because it's overcast, and well, the sun *does* cause cancer." The tall lady then giggled, with one finger held to her lips, as if she were a silly little pre-teen girl. Stacy noted how her voice seemed to be a bit high pitched, and in a concerted effort kind of way. What most folks might refer to as fake. The woman actually seemed to be speaking in *Italics!*

"Do you live around here?" Stacy asked.

"Kind of," the tall lady said, and she said it in a whisper, while leaning forward, as if where she lived was some sort of secret that one needed to have clearance from certain Government agencies before being allowed to know such undisclosed location.

"What's your name?" Stacy asked, trying not to sound off. She wasn't nervous. Stacy didn't get nervous. Despite being only thirty years old, and pretty, and petite, and looking much younger than she actually was, even though thirty was young enough, Stacy was one of the most brazen courtroom attorneys anyone twice her age, size and of the opposite gender had ever been. She was simply trying not to show this tall woman in front of her that she could tell she was being disingenuous. Stacy, obviously, was trying to make a better effort than the other woman to make a good first impression on her new neighbor.

"Oh," the woman said. "You can just call me Crazy A."

"Crazy A?" Stacy asked.

"Yeah," Crazy A said. "That's what everyone else calls me."

"I'm curious," Stacy said. "Why does everyone call you Crazy A?"

"Oh," Crazy A said, in a voice she was using to try to sound like a twelve year old girl again, rather than a woman in her mid-fifties, "because I'm silly."

Crazy A knew *not* to confuse Stacy with facts. Confusing people with facts was not her reproitare. Besides, if Crazy A were to be honest, something she seemed almost naturally to be incapable of, she'd have to tell Stacy that the real reason everyone called her Crazy A was because she was completely and insanely batshit crazy, and her first name starts with the letter A.

"Well, Crazy A," Stacy said. "I'd ask you how long you've been here, and maybe some other insignificant facts about yourself, solely for the purposes of small talk with a new neighbor, but if you can't even tell me if you live around here or not, I'm not so sure you could answer any other questions."

"Shame about what happened to the woman living here before you," Crazy A said, ignoring Stacy's comment and painting her best joker smile yet on her face. She could see that Stacy was a strong woman, though she'd sized her up at first glance to be anything but, because she was young, petite and pretty. She was going to be a tough nut to crack, Crazy A thought, but she would crack her. Crazy A cracked everyone.

"Yeah," Stacy said. "I got bits and pieces. Something about a bear attack. Seems like there's been a few of them around here."

"Yes," Crazy A said, trying to sound sad, and trying to whip up a crocodile tear or two, but that had never been her strength. That whole sociopathic slash can't feel real emotions thing she had going on kind of got in the way of crying. "Believe it or not," she continued, putting her head down, "my previous husband- I'm remarried now- died the same way."

"Of a bear attack?" Stacy said.

"Yes," Crazy A said, pausing for effect. She'd learned years before that though she couldn't cry, because she was a sociopath, she could pause for effect. "But I've moved on. I'm remarried. To an arborist. And actually, I do live just down the road from you."

"Oh," Stacy said, thinking perhaps the woman just lacked social skills, or had been a nerd since birth. "Which way?"

"Just down there," Crazy A said, pointing to the right as if heading out of Stacy's driveway. "As a matter of fact, I'd better be on my way. The clouds might disperse, and I'd hate to get skin cancer."

"Thanks for stopping by," Stacy said. "You're actually the first neighbor I've met."

"Sure," Crazy A said. "Stop by sometime."

"I will," Stacy said, and then she turned and walked back up the steps of her porch, and she sat back down and stared into the forest surrounding her home, and she thought of how Crazy A just ranked at the top of the strangest people she'd ever met in her life list.

Oh, and she made a mental note to keep an eye out for rabid bears.

***

The first couple of weeks in her new house had flown by for Stacy. No moss, grass, or even anything that might grow faster than moss or grass grew under her feet. In the past two weeks, not only had she gotten all her things unpacked and properly arranged, but she had also won two big court cases, and she celebrated all of it by going out and getting herself that brand new Trek road bike she'd been wanting. Especially, since she now lived out in the country part of the county, and no longer in the city, where cycling was much harder, and not as safe to do.

Stacy had gotten a late start on her Saturday morning bike ride, so when she was almost home, the sun was already up, and it was a typical hot, Virginia summer day. Stacy, when less than a mile away from her new home that we're ignoring the fact about the bank actually owning, she just happened to glance to her right, and up a long driveway and in the front yard a large, beautiful home, she saw Crazy A.

"That couldn't have been her," Stacy said to herself. The woman she'd just seen up in the yard was sunbathing. She was even holding one of those silver, reflective cardboard looking things that reflexes the sunlight back into your face. "I thought she was scared of the sun?"

Stacy turned around and went back and risked being shot by the property owner by biking up the drive. It was an upscale place, but still, it was Virginia.

"Hi there," Stacy said. The woman laying in the sun dropped the reflective panel she held in her hands and stared at Stacy. "It's me. Stacy. The new girl from just down the road."

"I'm sorry," Crazy A said. "Who?"

"Stacy," Stacy said, feeling confused. Had the woman forgotten her already? Was she actually older than her mid-fifties and had just aged well? Was she entering senility? "I just bought the house down the road."

Crazy A lowered one side of her sunglasses and stared hard. "I'm sorry," she said. "I don't remember you."

Stacy said nothing, because she could think of nothing to say. Was this tall, unattractive woman who had gone out of her way to speak like a twelve year old high on drugs? Was she drunk? Was she schizophrenic?

"Nice meeting you though," Crazy A said, putting her shades back on fully and then reclining back and raising her reflective panel in order to soak up the sun. "Have a good day."

Stacy tried to figure out just what the hell was going on on her way back home, but she just figured some people were nuts, and she'd just met another fitting the criteria.

Until that evening.

Stacy was sitting on her new porch participating in her one unhealthy habit. She was binge eating ice cream. She sat in her favorite wicker chair with an entire quart and a half sized container of Eddy's double fudge brownie on her lap. She was eating away, enjoying her nasty pleasure, when a car came up her driveway.

It was Crazy A.

"I'm sorry," Crazy A said, sticking her head out the window. She was rocking the twelve year old girl voice again, speaking in Italics and all. "I thought you said your name was Tracy."

"What?" Stacy said, confused.

"When you came by earlier," Crazy A said, unnecessarily raising her voice, as if attempting to be heard over the car's engine. There was no need. It was a Prius hybrid. You couldn't hear the engine. "I thought when we met that you said your name was Tracy. I was just confused."

"I thought you were scared of the sun," Stacy said, laughing afterward, thinking it must have been an honest mistake- the whole Stacy Tracy thing. "I'm glad to see you were just joking."

"What ever would make you think I was scared of the sun?" Crazy A asked from her car, still speaking unnecessarily loudly, and in Italics, in the voice of a twelve year old girl.

"When you were out walking," Stacy said. "The day you stopped by. You said you only went out when it was overcast, because the sun causes cancer."

"That's *crazy*," Crazy A said.

"Well," Stacy said. "That's what I thought, but I didn't want to say anything.

"Who would say such a thing," Crazy A said. "Only walking because it was overcast? Scared of the sun? I'm sure I said something entirely different, and you're just confused."

And instantly, Stacy *did* feel confused. Had she misheard Crazy A?

"Anyway," Crazy A said, "I'm off. It appears you and I share the same guilty pleasure. And I'm out. I'm off to the store."

"How's that?" Stacy said, confused more.

"Icecream," Crazy A said, pointing at the Eddy's in Stacy's hands. "I am so addicted to ice cream that I actually went out and bought a separate deep freezer for my home, just to store ice cream in. When there's a sale, I'll, honest to God, buy dozens of containers of it, because I eat ice cream, literally, everyday. No idea how I allowed myself to run so low without restocking, but oh well," Crazy A raised her palms to the sky and rolled her eyes. "I told you I was silly. So it happened."

"What's your favorite kind?" Stacy asked.

"Eddy's double fudge brownie," Crazy A said.

"Mine, too," Stacy said, holding up her container.

"I saw that," Crazy A said. "See you next time Stacy, whose name isn't Tracy," and then she giggled like a little girl and put the car in reverse and began backing down the driveway.

"See you next time, Crazy A who isn't really crazy, just silly," Stacy said, waving, feeling much better about the misunderstandings and confusions being cleared up.

Until two weeks later.

When Stacy ran into Crazy A in the grocery store.

***

The last two weeks had flown by as quickly as the two weeks before them had for Stacy, and she found herself at the grocery store, restocking on ice cream herself now, among other things. She was probably going to have a six pack of Northern Lights IPA after the conversation she'd just had with her mother over the phone on the way to the store. When Stacy had mentioned how fast time was flying by, her mother had given her the old "yes, and before you know it, you won't be young and pretty anymore, and no decent looking man will have you, and I'll never have any grandbabies," speech again. Stacy had miraculously driven into a dead zone (at least that's what she said before hanging up on her mother) and felt the urge to drink now, which was rare for her.

"Crazy A," Stacy said, seeing her new neighbor in the beer aisle as she made her way around the corner. "How are you?"

Crazy A stared at Stacy like she'd never seen her before and said nothing. She wasn't pretending to not know her, like before, but it did seem as if she was putting off the vibe of not dignifying Stacy's greeting with a greeting in return.

"I've got mine," Stacy said, reaching into her shopping cart and pulling out her quart and a half container of Eddy's double fudge brownie. "Have you picked yours up yet?"

"Picked up my what?" Crazy A said, monotone.

"Your ice cream," Stacy said, still smiling. "You really are silly."

"We don't eat ice cream," Crazy A said. "I haven't eaten ice cream since I was a child."

"What?" Stacy said, feeling the exact same way she had when Crazy A had acted like she couldn't remember meeting her. And when she said she'd never claimed to be scared of the sun. Was this woman, this Crazy A character suffering from multiple personalities? Or was Stacy, herself, losing her mind. "You said this was your favorite," Stacy said, raising the ice cream higher. "You said you bought a freezer just for ice cream."

"Ice cream," Crazy A began, "and other dairy products, causes very painful kidney stones." She said it so matter of factly, Stacy was truly now doubting her own sanity. "My brother in law," Crazy A continued, "had a kidney stone several years ago, because he was eating too much ice cream, and he went through absolute agony passing it. It made me thank my lucky stars for not having eaten ice cream in forty years, and there's no way I'd start eating it now." And with that, Crazy A pushed her cart along, and went on her way, and left Stacy standing there in the beer aisle, her ice cream in hand and her shopping cart half filled.

Stacy put her ice cream back in her cart and decided on a twelve pack instead of a six pack. As she was hefting the box of beer out of the cooler and putting it into her cart, an older woman approached her and said hello.

"Hi," Stacy said, turning to make eye contact with the woman.

"I just saw all that," the woman said. She appeared to be in her seventies, yet still very attractive. She was wearing rubber gloves. The type dentists wear. When the woman noticed Stacy staring at her hands, she spoke again. "Look," she said. "I have OCD. I'm kind of a germaphobe. But I know it, and I get help. Not everyone who knows they're sick does, and I'm afraid you just dealt with one of the sickest people you could ever meet in your life."

"You mean Crazy A?" Stacy said.

"Yes," the older woman said. "Completely insane, batshit Crazy A."

Stacy was not a gossiper, but she didn't tell this woman as much, because she wanted to hear what she had to say.

"I don't like to talk about others behind their back," the older woman said when she spoke again, "but I feel it's my duty to tell you about Crazy A."

***

They say that in life, things happen in threes. Obviously, much is the same for marginally average written short stories, because two weeks later, (this being the third two weeks long period to pass in this story in a row between Stacy and Crazy A's meetings), here came Crazy A, running frantically up Stacy's driveway, screaming something incoherent, as Stacy sat on her porch, eating ice cream, because she loved it so much, and drinking beer, because she'd just gotten off of the phone with her mother. She figured she'd blow out all the excessive carbs and calories on tomorrow morning's bike ride.

And Stacy was ready for Crazy A and her bullshit this time!

The old woman that Stacy had met in the grocery store two weeks before, when Crazy A had denied ever eating ice cream, even though, just two weeks before that she'd claimed to have gone out and bought a deep freezer exclusively for ice cream, had been Crazy A's previous neighbor some time ago. The woman had lived across the road from Crazy A and her then husband, a man everyone referred to as Jittery J, back before Jittery J was mauled to death by a bear. Or at least that's how the *official* story went; that Jittery J had been mauled to death by a *bear*.

The old lady had invited Stacy to her home for a beer, and over more than just one, the old lady gave Stacy the skinny on Crazy A.

"It's called gaslighting," the old woman said, when she began explaining Crazy A's personality disorder.

To Stacy's understanding, from what the old lady told her, gaslighters are people who *do* have a personality disorder, known as gaslighting, and they *are* very much aware of it, but they choose to do nothing about it, because it's really an outward behavior induced by other disorders, mostly narcissism based on deep rooted insecurity and an antisocial personality disorder.

Gaslighters are knowingly manipulative. They will intentionally switch their stories around on you each time they see you, or, as Crazy A had done with Stacy, act as if they had no recollection of having said what they had said in the first place, which is basically the same thing. Many gaslighters will act like an event occurred that never did. They'll passive aggressively insult someone, and when called out for it, say it wasn't what was meant, and act hurt, because the person took it the wrong way, however, the other person took it exactly how they meant it.

Gaslighters are the kings and queens of lies of omission. They'll intentionally lead their listener down a certain path when telling a story of an event that occurred, get them thinking they see how things are going to go, or how things went, and then stop, knowing that the path veered, but they do not want their listener, albeit, their victim, to know the facts. And then, if ever called out on having misled their listener, when and if they find out the path veered, and what really happened, they always shrug, eyes wide and the palms of their hands up, and say, "I never told you that. That's what you chose to believe."

Some gaslighters will go as far as to claim to see things that aren't even there, all in order to get their victim, who obviously cannot see what they claim to be there, because it isn't there, to question their own sanity.

"It's all done to gain the power of control over someone," the old lady had told Stacy.

"Why would some random woman down the road," Stacy asked, "a neighbor at that, want to control me?"

"Because she has no control anywhere else in her life," the old woman had informed her. She explained how Crazy A was born into money, and instead of going out and doing anything meaningful with her life, she had done the bare minimum to keep Mommy and Daddy happy, so as not to get cut off. "She became part of the idle wealthy," as the woman put it. "And she simply has nothing better to do than go around gaslighting people. It's like a hobby. Or used to be, anyway. Sadly, it's become her way of life. She actually gets her rocks off from doing it."

The woman explained how so many of their other neighbors had had to learn the hard way, but most had gotten word from the others before they got too deep into thinking they were losing their minds at the hands of Crazy A's manipulation. Crazy A had actually moved just miles down the road, in the past, the old woman further informed Stacy, simply to have new neighbors she could gaslight, because her existing neighbors had figured her out and there was simply no more gaslighting excitement in her life.

"You're telling me this woman has moved, only miles away from her existing, perfectly good house, just to have new neighbors to gaslight?" Stacy said, knowing she'd heard some crazy shit in the courtroom before, but rarely, anything this crazy.

"Honey," the older woman said to Stacy. "Do you have any idea why everyone calls her Crazy A?"

"She told me it was because she was silly," Stacy said, "but I obviously know differently now."

"Yes," the old woman said. "It's because the truth is, the woman is completely and insanely batshit crazy, and her name starts with the letter A."

"Does anyone know what her real name is?" Stacy asked.

"Oh," the old woman said, in a voice sounding as if she was trying to remember something from long ago. "We used to. But we forgot."

The old woman went on to explain that there is only one way to deal with a gaslighter. You had to cut them off immediately by calling them out on their bullshit. The best way of doing it was to laugh, obnoxiously and loudly, at their next attempt of gaslighting and flat out tell them that you do not believe them. Burst their facade forcefully and immediately.

Further, the old woman explained, you must then insult them. Tell them you know they're full of shit, and that you've known they were full of shit the whole time and that you were simply trying to be friendly, but that you're not going to buy their shit anymore. Tell them that you know the truth. They're liars, they're losers who've never accomplished anything, hence the deep rooted insecurities that led to the gaslighting, and no matter what, under no circumstances- no matter how badly doing this to someone else makes you feel- you do *not* go back at a later date and apologize to the gaslighter. Gaslighters don't want help and they never stop gaslighting. It's the only way to a sense of power or authority that they have access to, and they will view any apology as a weakness, and they will use it as a door to get back into your life and your head and start gaslighting again.

"Wow," Stacy said after hearing the solution to her problem with Crazy A. "It sounds like gaslighters live lonely lives."

"They do," the old woman said. "But that's their preference. That's where that whole antisocial personality part comes in. Honestly, they hate most other people and have no use for them unless it's for personal gain. But they know this sort of attitude is not accepted in society, so they fake it. They act kind. They play nice. They come across as friendly. But underneath, they're planning their psychological attack on you. Gaslighters are some of the sickest mother fuckers you'll ever meet in your life, and I consider myself a lady, and I can't remember that last time I used that term, mother fucker."

"Wow!" Stacy said. Her mind had been blown.

But the talk had prepared Stacy, and she was ready, so as Crazy A came at her, running up the driveway, screaming something about something, Stacy stood to her feet, and...

...she started laughing.

Hysterically.

"Nice, try," Stacy said. "But I'm not buying it, you lying bitch."

"Help me," Crazy A said. "We have to get inside. We're going to be killed. We have to get inside."

Crazy A reached the foot of the steps leading up the porch, but Stacy had raced down them, and she confronted Crazy A face to face at the bottom of the steps. "You are not welcome in my house, or on my property, anymore, for that matter," Stacy said. "You are a lying, manipulative gaslighting bitch, and I'm calling you out." And then she laughed again for good measure.

"There's a fucking Bigfoot Sasquatch in the woods by the side of the road," Crazy A said, putting on the best act, as Stacy saw it, anyone could. Hell, if Crazy A had applied herself in life, Stacy thought, she could have been an actress. She really did seem terrified. Stacy, for just a second, thought there might be a Bigfoot Sasquatch in the woods. "We have to get in the fucking house, now!"

"Likely story," Stacy said, smiling, and still laughing. "Look, you lying sack of crap," she continued. "I know all about you. I talked with one of your old neighbors. I know who and what you are."

"We are going to be killed," Crazy A screamed. "Look!" she turned and pointed. "There's a fucking Bigfoot Sasquatch coming up your fucking driveway to kill us!"

"I'm not even going to dignify that bullshit story by turning my head to look anywhere in that direction," Stacy said, proud of herself to be acting on the advice Crazy A's old neighbor had given her. And she didn't even try to sneak a glance at the driveway. "Leave, and do *not* come back."

Stacy turned and began walking up her porch steps. Crazy A grabbed her by the back of the shoulder and tried to go with her.

Bam!

Stacy turned and punched Crazy A so hard on the chin, an upper-cut (it had to be, because Crazy A was so much taller than Stacy), and it knocked Crazy A flat on her back.

"You touched me first, bitch! I'm a lawyer, and I know the rules, so try to sue me," is all that Stacy said before continuing in the house and slamming and locking the door.

***

Just as Stacy was opening her door to go to work the next morning, she was met on the other side of the door by Burt Reynolds, a local lawman.

"Shit," Stacy said. She knew Burt, from work, and wasn't shy to be herself in front of him. "That bitch is actually going to try to sue me? She touched me first?"

"What bitch, Stacy?" Burt asked.

"Crazy A."

"Crazy A can't sue you," Burt said.

"I know, right?" Stacy said. "She touched me first."

"Stacy," Burt said. "Crazy A is dead."

"What?" Stacy said. "What happened?"

"Not sure yet," he said, trying not to let it show that he was afraid he may know a little too much. A little more than he could say without getting locked up in the nuthouse. "A jogger reported the body this morning just after daybreak. Saw her body strung out in the woods about twenty feet off the road. Just down here below your driveway. I was just coming up to ask you if you saw or heard anything strange yesterday evening, just before dark."

"She was here," Stacy said, now feeling like a real piece of shit for treating Crazy A the way she had. "She was frantic. She said something was chasing her."

"Why didn't you let her inside?" Burt asked.

"I didn't believe her," Stacy said. "I'd caught her up in a ton of lies, and I was actually breaking off our brief friendship." Stacy paused, looking down. "Burt, I had recently determined that the woman was completely and insanely batshit crazy, and having any sort of relationship with her was unhealthy, and I honest to God thought she was making up the whole being chased thing in order to weasel her way back into my life. Crazy people do that shit."

"Oh, I know," Burt said, agreeing. "I see some of the craziest stuff in law enforcement." Burt paused. And then he said, "Stacy? You got any idea what she said was chasing her?"

Stacy looked at Burt. Their eyes locked, and she felt as if he was reading her mind, but she also felt that if she told the truth, she'd be the one locked up in the nuthouse.

"A bear," she said, when she finally spoke. "I believe I remember her saying she'd seen a bear."

"A bear," Burt said, looking down, his hopes of Stacy being honest shattered. He might not have believed her had she been, but he could tell she was lying now. "Are you sure it wasn't something else?" He asked, looking up at her again.

"No," she said. "It was a bear."

"Thanks, Stacy," Burt said. "See you in court for that D.U.I. case you're defending this afternoon."

Burt walked down the porch steps and then down the driveway. His cruiser was still at the scene below, along with the other cruisers and an ambulance that should have been a hearse.

"Another fucking bear," Burt said to himself, feeling as if someday, he would eventually get to the truth.

But one thing was for sure.

Crazy A was no more.

She'd had a very unfortunate demise.

The End

Here's The Bigfoot Sasquatch Story You'll Never Hear Me Tell On YouTube

Some people get it, and some people don't. I'll never understand why so many people suffer from black and white thinking. It's got to be this, or it's got to be that, and there's absolutely *no* room for a gray area in the middle. At least that's what *they* think.

These black and white thinkers can be broken down into subcategories, too. There are too many to mention, but the ones that stand out on our YouTube channel are the ones who think that if you make one humorous video on your YouTube channel, perhaps one with a giant spider (named, by the way, Ginormica Enormica, because it is both ginormous and enormous), then there is absolutely *no way* that any of your other videos were real, or that you were being serious in them, and there's even an old Roman expression, they'll tell you, which states that once you're caught in a falsehood once, you are to never be taken seriously or trusted again.

And then, there is the subcategory of black and white thinkers who believe that if you are unwilling to pick a side- either with those *do* definitely believe in Bigfoot Sasquatch, or with those who definitely do *not* believe in Bigfoot Sasquatch- then you are obviously making fun of one of the two sides, if not both. This whole idea of thinking that maybe, just maybe, some huge, two legged creature which no one has ever provided hardcore proof of existing might or might not exist, is ludicrous, these people think. How dare you not take sides, they scream. This is America (at least where I am, and thank you to our international readers and viewers for being here, we know there are many of you), and by God we pick sides here in America so we can agree with our sidemates and hate the people on the other side. That's what America is all about!

But then there's the truth.

Potentially.

Some of the behind the scenes stuff that you don't see on camera, because it is intentionally left out.

For protection.

And not just for the safety of me and my beautiful family, but potentially, for...

...him, her, it or they.

***

By the second half of 2019 we were getting close. I mean, really, really close. As close as what appeared to be about forty yards away in one of our videos.

Close to what? You ask?

Potentially, him, her, it or they, of course.

We'd captured several oddities in several of our videos recently that simply could not be explained. Months and months of refining my own, unique Bigfoot Sasquatch researching methods were appearing to pay off. All those construction paper cutouts. Strapping gopro cameras to my head. The fake hillbilly teeth and the miles upon endless miles of hiking and recording footage in the beautiful Blue Ridge Mountains of Virginia, sometimes in below freezing temperatures during winter, and sometimes with the heat index over one hundred in the summer. It was all culminating to the point of what may or may not be living in the woods behind my home allowing us to get closer.

Potentially.

Him, her, it or they were getting closer to us.

Potentially.

And then, in late October, just one week before Halloween, we may or may not have filmed, arguably, *the best* Bigfoot Sasquatch footage that currently exists on the internet!

Potentially.

And that's when it happened.

I do not JADE, though I have a very long history of doing so. JADE is when we 'justify, argue, defend, or explain' our points, our actions, our decisions to someone, either because we feel the need to do so, or because they *demand* we do so, and for some reason we cave to their demands and just start JADE'ing away.

Guilt and shame are two of the most useless emotions human beings can have. Sure, there's remorse- honestly being sorry for your words or actions- and remorse is good, especially when you combine some amends or even restitution with it if possible and if necessary. But after that, it's time to move onward and upward. It's called the healing process. To sit around and stew in guilt and shame is counterproductive. It is the opposite of healing, and it is futile.

And anyone who thinks that's where you should be? By continuously asking you to JADE?

Does not belong in your life.

No matter who they are!

Period.

No potentially about it.

What does this psychobabble have to do with Bigfoot Sasquatch? And this story?

A lot!

So, when you work in social media, especially around this topic, you often get two types of people or groups that JADE you, some of them even crossing lines most sane people would not cross. These groups or individuals want to either come out and confirm what you may or may not have found, or they want to come out and debunk you. The end goal of these groups or individuals, whichever their goal is, is basically rooted in the same reason.

They want to get the credit for your work if you were right.

Or they want to get famous for debunking your work if you were wrong.

Self centered egomaniacs who see you as opportunity, either way.

After publishing the video from October of 2019, where we may or may not have actually filmed him, her, it or they, I began getting even more emails and messages on our YouTube channel, Homesteading Off The Grid, by way of the comment section from these sorts of groups and individuals, and there was one group in particular, who will not be named, because I would never want to give them any free advertising, who thought their name and their popularity in the Bigfoot Sasquatch community would guarantee me returning their messages and actually meeting up with them, here, at my family's home, and that I would willingly take them on a personal tour and show them, exactly, where the potential lair of Bigfoot Sasquatch was.

Wrong!

Not to JADE, nay, *NEVER* to JADE, but I get completely dumbfounded by the number of people who don't stop to consider, for even a moment, that our homestead, this beautiful property that may appear to be a stage of our YouTube channel, is not a stage, but an actual, bonafide home.

Our home!

Who, in their right mind, watches someone on YouTube, a complete stranger who they never have, nor would probably never meet, and contact them and ask if they can come meet with them?

Nutcases!

That's who!

And we get it all the time. People who want to come camping on our property. People who want to go Bigfoot Sasquatch hunting with us. Oh, it would make your skin crawl if you saw all the messages we get in this regard. Most of them get held in the 'potentially inappropriate' filter on YouTube, so I'm able to ban the nutcases and their messages never appear on the channel publicly.

So, anyway, this particular group, who thought they were *somebody*, obviously didn't take a liking to me not returning their emails and replying to their comments.

So they actually freaking started coming by!

I shit you not!

These people had the audacity to contact me, after I'd never returned any of their messages, and told me that I might have the right to ignore them and keep them off of *my* property, but they by God had the right to contact people who lived around me and ask permission to go on *their* properties. They let me know that they knew all about the annoying neighbor I'd run off with a crayon, and that they were sure he wouldn't mind them actually setting up camp on his mommy and daddy's property so they could pull surveillance on mine.

Further, they let me know that they'd be watching, soon, and that when I took off to go back to the potential lair of Bigfoot Sasquatch, they'd be following, and whether I liked it or not, I would lead them right to him, her, it, or they, and they would forever be remembered as being the group who could provide undeniable proof of the existence of him, her, it, or they.

Or that they were going to destroy my career!

***

It's not hard to tell when someone's casing your house. Especially when you live out in the middle of nowhere, like we do, and especially after you've lived there long enough to be familiar with pretty much any vehicle that passes by your house on any sort of regular basis, like we have. Sure, we get plenty of touristy types passing through, especially in the fall, people who are driving around aimlessly, looking at the leaves, because it's simply so beautiful out here in the fall, but there's nothing much touristy about jacked up four wheel drive Jeeps and trucks with giant satellite dishes and dogs in the back of them.

So the first one I noticed was a Jeep with two guys, driving by my house one late morning, just before noon. The vehicle stuck out like a sore thumb, due to what appeared to be a giant satellite dish in the back. "Look at that Jeep," I said to my beautiful bride, Dearly, a.k.a. 'Giggly Girl,' as it passed by the first time. "I bet those are those Bigfoot Sasquatch people from that one group I'll never name and give free advertising to."

She just giggled and called me crazy.

But I didn't seem so crazy when I saw them going back the other way about ten minutes later. She wasn't giggling anymore, either. Because she wasn't there. She'd gone in the house. But had she been out there, she would have giggled, because that's what she does. She giggles, just like Jittery J used to jitter before having his unfortunate demise in volume 1 of this series.

Over the next few days, I would see several four wheel drive trucks, not muddy, quite clean on the contrary, and they seemed to be loaded down with camping gear and equipment. None of these people ever tried to approach me, and I'm sure it's because they knew they'd get a big fat no if they asked to come on my land or for me to guide them to the lair.

After about a week or so, I was convinced I was paranoid, and that it had to be ludicrous to think that any of these people driving around my place, back and forth, all day it seemed, had anything to do with the messages I'd received from the group I'll not name. Who the hell did I think *I* was? I'm not that important. Sure, we've got a pretty hefty loyal following of folks on our YouTube channel, but would this organization actually mobilize and deploy units to my central Virginia homestead? Besides, it *is* hunting season that time of year, and I was probably just seeing the vehicles of people who live outside of our area who'd come here to hunt.

Nine days after I'd originally captured the footage I may or may not have captured on the video I recorded at the end of October, I decided I'd head back up into the potential Bigfoot Sasquatch lair and see if I could have a repeat performance. I hadn't seen the guys in trucks for a few days, so I figured I'd waited them out and they'd gone back to wherever they'd come from. Or, they had been hunters, and they'd bagged their limit, and they were back in their cubicles at work lying to their coworkers about how big the deer they'd gotten the week before was. Hey, I used to hunt deer, and I'd turned many of little spikes into raging twelve pointers the size of moose back in my days of lying about deer hunting.

There are many ways to enter the area I refer to as the potential lair of Bigfoot Sasquatch, and I wasn't in the mood to walk forever that day, because I'd run a 5k road race that morning, my first road race in roughly fifteen years, and I was already tired, and I was in a foul mood after having been beaten in the race by so many women in their sixties and 20 year old college girls. I used to be a pretty good runner, and I was always racing, and I have no idea how all of a sudden, after having been away from the sport for so long, all these older ladies and young girls got so damn fast, but they have.

Anyway, I really stretched that video out. I think it was thirty minutes long. It wasn't intentional. I'd taken some pepperoni and fried chicken with me, and I was really just letting off steam in regard to my disappointment about the race, and I couldn't see any large, dark objects moving on the screen behind my back, where my six o'clock is, but I knew the video had gone on too long, so I wrapped it up and headed back out of the lair. I'd driven to one of the few places you could park at the foot of the mountain, and I'll be damned if when I got down there, I didn't see that funky looking Jeep and a couple of the four wheel drive trucks that had been passing by my house nearly two weeks before.

Some of the vehicles had people in them and some didn't. I assumed they had people out in the woods trying to see where I was, and others were watching from the vehicles to see which direction I'd exit the woods from, so they'd get a better sense of where the lair might be.

It took some time and some stealth, but I actually walked away from the parking area and went down the road, hidden in the woods, quite a way, and then I cross the road and came back up through the woods, so that when I exited the woods, I did so from the opposite side of the road I'd actually been on. It worked, as when I got in my vehicle, and I watched what these people were doing by the use of my mirrors, I could see that they weren't wasting any time in jumping out of their vehicles and gearing up and heading up into the woods I'd just exited.

Again, I might have just been paranoid, but I was convinced that I was being watched by a group of Bigfoot Sasquatch hunters, and the last thing I was going to do was lead them straight to where I may or may not have captured one of these creatures on video.

So I did not return to the potential lair of Bigfoot Sasquatch for months!

And I devised a plan.

Over the next few months, I nearly completely lost any credibility I may have built up in the Bigfoot Sasquatch community (and yes, I know that sounds like an oxymoron, and I love it, but it doesn't mean I'm making fun of anyone, damn it!) by making some of the most insane, asinine, and yes, fake videos that anyone could imagine making. Come on, if you're reading this, I know you probably watch my videos on Homesteading Off The Grid, on YouTube, so you know *exactly* which videos I'm talking about. You saw them. They were so obviously fake.

And I regret none of it.

Not only have I never set out to find Bigfoot Sasquatch for fame and glory, I never set out to find him, her, it, or they in the first place. If you've made it to volume three in this soon to be 100 volume series (well, maybe not so soon), then you know from the story I told in volume 1, we never asked for this nightmare. We were simply making videos about corn and green beans, and some really strange things were going on around our homestead, and sometimes, we'd unintentionally capture it on video.

With this said, there is one thing that I *am* definitely all about, and that is keeping these beautiful creatures, if they do indeed exist, and if they are what is actually coming around here and causing strange things to happen on our property, completely hidden. I don't need proof, and I know that at the hands of proof comes lots of destruction.

And dissection!

I can only imagine the damage that the Government and the scientific community would dish out on any population of any previously undiscovered species that resembles mankind to such a great degree. I'm sure it would all be done in the name of potentially finding a cure for cancer or Covid-19 or whatever, but these beautiful creatures would suffer, and I never liked the idea of lab test animals, and this is exactly what he, she, it or they would become.

Now, were the videos I made during this several months long period entertaining? Of course. Were they fun to make? Absolutely. And did I care about losing credibility? Not at all. I never knew I had any in the first place. Come on, this is cryptozoology, not biology. We're pseudoscientists, people.

But I do take great pride in knowing that I waited out those folks from that group that will not be named here. They all of a sudden, around the end of December, just before Christmas, stopped coming around. I never saw that Jeep with the satellite dish in the back and all those jacked up four wheel drive trucks again.

And I began, very erratically and over very dispersed time periods, going back into the potential lair of Bigfoot Sasquatch.

And most times, I never take my camera.

Oh, the things I see on those trips.

But who would believe me now? After destroying any credibility I might have once had?

So I'll just keep those moments where they belong.

Between me and him, her, it or they.

The End

The Tale Of The Bladeless Riding Lawn Mower Thieving Bladeless Riding Lawn Mower Riding Bigfoot Sasquatch!

I never thought that if I lived to be one hundred that I would come to believe there can be times when writer's block does not suck, but I am now a convinced man, because this story will detail, exactly, how if I had not been suffering from writer's block on one super hot summer day in Virginia, none of us would have ever gotten to hear the tale of the bladeless riding lawn mower thieving bladeless riding lawn mower riding bigfoot sasquatch!

Mark Twain put it best, the way he told the story in his book 'Roughing It.' You know the one. If you don't, you should read it. It was about his experiences when he went out west to try to get rich during the silver rush. In it, he details the time he got a job as an editor for a newspaper. At first, he loved it, because editor is a pretty important position. Editors are important people. They're much like college professors, in that they know all there is to know in their respective fields, in this case, the editor's field being writing, but for some reason, just like college professors and their respective fields, with all their knowledge on the subject, they're not any good at it.

But the point I'm trying to make here, a point that Twain made better than anyone else could, is in regard to content. Story. And the sheer amount of it.

Twain spoke of how you could be a really great writer, and write one really great book, and never have to work again and be remembered forever. J.D. Salinger, author of "Catcher in the Rye" comes to mind here. Salinger wrote one book in his life, and it just happened to be one of the best books ever written (be sure to read that one, too, if you haven't), and BAM! Just like that, he was done.

But an editor? Man, you have to come up with an editorial piece every single day. Twain, and he might have been exaggerating when he said this, and he might have just been trying to draw out the length of his story to make sure it was full length novel length (that's forty thousand words or more, by the way), because that 'ol rascal was known to do such things, but he said, that if you think about it, if a man or a woman were to be an editor of a paper for a full thirty year career span, they probably, over that period of thirty years, write enough words to fill a library.

And I believe him.

And he didn't last long as an editor. But fortunately for those of us who love a good story, well told, we remember that 'ol rascal.

So what does this have to do with writer's block? And the tale of the bladeless riding lawn mower thieving bladeless riding lawn mower riding bigfoot sasquatch? Well, I'm getting there, but I gotta tell it in order, and no, I'm not pulling a Mark Twain on you.

Potentially.

So, I'm no editor for any newspaper, though I used to work for several, but I am what you might call a modern day jack of all trades kind of guy when it comes to writing. I write books, like this one, a series of short story collections, and I write full length novels. Off and on, throughout the years, I've been a journalist, I've been a blogger, and I also have my YouTube channel which is really like writing in video form. I don't write any scripts for the channel, though many vertically challenged individuals who live under bridges often comment on the videos, stating that they appear to be scripted (I think they may be trying to compliment me, because the video came off so well it had to be planned out by professionals, but I'm not sure), but they're not.

So I was up in this super hot room where I write, on a super hot day in July, staring at the laptop, and not a single word would come to me. I'd been working on the next Bigfoot Sasquatch Files collection, the one you're reading now, as well as what I honestly believe will be remembered as my masterpiece, long after I'm gone. It's a collection of thirty one short stories, three thousand to six thousand words long each, like the stories in the Bigfoot Sasquatch Files series, and it's for the Halloween season, as all of the stories are paranormal, supernatural, and all around creepy in nature.

I'd been writing up to five thousand words a day (that's the equivalent of roughly twenty five pages in a book), and I was burned the hell out.

So I went fishing.

I've learned that when the words won't come, they just aren't going to come, and you just can't force them. You'll end up writing a bunch of crap that no one will like. This can be said with any form of work. If your heart's not in it, people can tell.

My beautiful bride Dearly, a.k.a. Giggly Girl and our son, Daniel, were off on a playdate with Daniel's best friend and his best friend's mother, so I didn't have my family here to go fishing with me, but I went anyway, something I rarely do. I just viewed it as if I'd be having a *me* day, something I do even more rarely.

It was ninety five degrees outside, with a heat index of one hundred, so I let the truck's air conditioner cool the cab down a bit before I actually jumped in and took off. I knew it was too hot to fish, and I didn't expect to catch anything, but a bad day fishing is always better than a good day at work, hell, even if the words *are* coming, so I went anyway, as soon as the truck's cab cooled down.

I got to one of my favorite spots on the Rivanna River in Charlottesville, but the air conditioning in the truck felt so good, and the outside temps were still so high, that I decided I didn't want to get out of the truck just yet so I just kept going. The next thing I know, I was in Scottsville, down in the southern part of Albemarle county, now riding along the banks of the James River, and it was still so damn hot, I didn't want to get out, so I just kept going, still.

I entered into Buckingham County, which is the geographic center of the state of Virginia, and I thought, well, I guess I am literally in the middle of nowhere now, and the temperature had dropped to ninety, so I decided I'd wet a line (that means go fishing for those of you reading this who are not from the south). I found a public boat loading area on the James and parked in the parking lot. I took my rod and tackle and my can of worms upstream, around the bend, so as not to interfere with or be disturbed by any boaters. I found a huge sycamore tree (those are the largest trees east of the Mississippi River, by the way), that provided plenty of shade, so I set up shop and started fishing.

"You done beat me to it," I heard a voice say, downstream from me, about ten minutes after I'd cast my line and sat down on one of the giant Sycamore roots protruding through the sandy bank and started sweating profusely. I looked downstream, and about twenty yards away was an older black gentleman coming my way with four rods and a chair and a can of worms in his hands. Once upon a time I would have referred to him as an old gentleman, because he was about sixty years old, but since I'm almost fifty, I've started using the term older instead of old, and I hope others will pay me the same respect.

"There's enough shade under this big ol' sycamore for both of us," I said.

"I reckon there is," he said. If you're not from the south, "reckon" means think."

He came under the tree with me and introduced himself as Michael. I told him my name, and then he went up about fifteen yards away from me and wet all four of his lines, then he sat back in that folding chair he'd brought with him and started sweating profusely. "Too danged hot to be a fishin' today," he said, and I agreed with him, and we both just kept on fishing.

Michael and I talked off and on for a bit. It was so damned hot it was even too hot to talk for too long. Every now and then, we'd see a catfish drifting by, riding the current, and they'd look over at our baited hooks, and we could tell they really wanted to go over there and eat those worms, but you see, fish are cold blooded animals, which means their body temperatures are whatever the temperature of their surroundings are, and as hungry as those catfish were, and as good as they thought our worms looked, it was just too damned hot for them to make the effort of swimming over there to eat the worms. And it's a damn shame, because some of them were among the biggest catfish I'd ever seen!

I guess those catfish just kept on riding that current, not putting forth any effort, and they probably made it down close to Richmond before the water temperatures cooled down enough to where they could swim without being miserable at night.

"You think those things spend all night swimming back up stream just to get home after drifting all the way down to Richmond during the day?" I asked Michael, since we'd gotten to talking about it and all. "And then just float all the way back down to Richmond the next day?"

"I reckon they do," Michael said. "In this heat. L'awd knows it's too damn hot to fish on a day like this." I agreed with him again and we both kept fishing.

As the hours passed, and man, do they pass slowly during the heat of these Virginia summers, the temperatures actually began to drop noticeably. The sun went back behind the horizon, we began sweating less profusely, and I could have sworn, some of those giant catfish started actually flapping their fins on one side, in hopes of making it over to our worms on hooks. We were able to start talking a little more, without getting worn out from the heat, and when Michael asked me what kind of work I did (he was a retired clerk from the post office, by the way), I told him. I explained just how much I write, and how I'd been writing up to five thousand words a day, and that I was suffering from writer's block so badly, I knew there was no way I could sit down and pump out a story that would be any good, nothing anyone would want to read, so even though it was hotter than hell's unairconditioned outhouse I decided to go fishing.

"What you trying to write about?" Michael asked.

"Bigfoot Sasquatch," I said, and man, did he start laughing so hard, he didn't *almost* fall out of his chair, he *did* fall out of his chair. I jumped up and went over to help him up, worried it might be heat related, or age related, because he wasn't old yet (wink, wink), but he *was* older. By the time I got to him, he'd gotten back up and got back in his chair, but he thanked me for my concern nonetheless and we both agreed we wished some of those giant catfish in the James River there, floating down to Richmond would make a similar effort for our worms.

"I wadn't laughin' at you," Michael said. "It's just that I've only heard one other person in my life refer to it as Bigfoot Sasquatch, rather than either or, and it's been years since I've heard it."

"Who else used to call it (or him, or her, or they) Bigfoot Sasquatch?" I asked, intrigued.

"Oh," Michael began, looking down at his feet, recalling a memory. "Just some crazy ol' white man."

"How is it that you know of this crazy 'ol white man?" I asked. "It wouldn't be by way of YouTube, would it?"

"What?" Michael said, looking over at me now.

"YouTube," I said. "Do you watch this crazy 'ol white man on YouTube?"

"Naw," he said, looking back down at his feet. "I don't do that internet stuff. D'rather be fishing. Even on days like this, when it's too hot to fish." I agreed with him and we both kept fishing, and then he said, "back when I was a boy. Here in Buckingham County. Used to be this crazy ol' white guy, probably the age I am now, he was known for going on and on about a Bigfoot Sasquatch stealing his bladeless riding lawn mower and running off with it."

"What?" I said. "You've got to be kidding me."

"I kid you not," he said. "And the strangest thing is?" He took a pause for effect, which I've been told I'm really good at doing on my YouTube channel by those vertically challenged individuals who live under bridges who say my videos appear to be scripted, and then he said, "I believe him, because me and a buddy was there the night it happened, and we saw it."

"You've got to be kidding me," I said.

"I done told ya I wasn't a kiddin' ya," he said. "And I don't know what exactly it was that I saw, but I know I saw something."

"You've got to give me details," I said.

"Well," he said. "If'n these here temperatures drop about two more degrees, I might be able to tell it without putting myself out too much. It's just too hot to talk for long today, and it's definitely too hot to fish." I agreed with him, and we kept fishing, and we picked a log that was out in the river, about twenty yards away from the bank we were sitting on and about ten feet further away than any of those ginormous catfish that were drifting by us, riding the currents downstream where they'd just have to start swimming back upstream to make it home in the middle of the night once the temperatures dropped. We agreed that once the first catfish made it over to that log, enroute to our worm baited hooks, which were about ten yards on the other side of that log, Michael would tell me the tale of the bladeless lawn mower thieving bladeless lawn mower riding bigfoot sasquatch.

Now here's where things take a turn for the weird. This was only supposed to be a story about a *story* about a bigfoot sasquatch, but as we were sitting there waiting for the temperatures to drop, Michael and I both kept getting glimpses of what appeared to be a large, bipedal creature on the other side of the James River, and if that was, indeed, what we were seeing, then this would no longer be a story about a story about Bigfoot Sasquatch, but that would actually make this a bonafide Bigfoot Sasquatch story itself.

Potentially.

"So when I was about thirteen," Michael bagan. I guess he'd seen one of those humongous catfish drifting down to Richmond reach the log, which, technically, meant that lucky fish might have ended up only floating down to Scottsville before he'd start swimming for home around midnight, when the water temperatures dropped enough for him to make an effort without putting himself out too much. "That's when it happened. And again, I ain't gonna put my hand on no Bible that it was a Bigfoot Sasquatch, but my buddy and me done seen something."

"There was this crazy ol' white guy," Michael said. "I think his name was Roy. I can't remember, exactly, but I believe it was Roy."

"Sounds about right," I said, and Michael asked me what *that* meant, because I wasn't there, and I told him when I was a kid I knew an older (not old) white guy whose name was Roy, and he was lunatic. Michael saw my point, and he continued his story.

"So this crazy 'ol white guy, whose name I think was Roy," Michael said, "everywhere he went, he went on a riding lawn mower that didn't have a blade on it."

"Why didn't it have a blade on it?" I asked.

"Cause it was his primary form of transportation," Michael said. "It was like his car. He didn't use it to actually mow grass."

"Why didn't he just have a car?" I asked.

"Story I got," Michael said, "was that he'd had about twenty drinking and driving convictions and had lost his license for life."

"How the hell was he not in jail?" I asked.

"This was back in the late sixties," Michael said. "Hell, most people had a pile of D.U.I.'s back then. You just paid a fine and went on. It wasn't until the eighties when all these congressmen and senators' kids started getting killed by drunk drivers that they really started laying the hammer down."

"Oh," I said, thankful for the brief history lesson on drunk driving laws."

"So anyways," Michael continued, "You'd just see crazy 'ol Roy. Can we agree on his name being Roy? Just for this story?"

"Sure," I said. "I've already told you I knew an older white guy named Roy, and he was a complete nutcase, so it's fitting."

"So you'd see crazy 'ol Roy," Michael continued, "just ridin' that bladeless riding lawn mower everywhere. It wasn't really a town. You know we have the town of Dillwyn down here in Buckingham County, and even that ain't much of a town, but way out in the county where I growed up, we didn't even have anything like Dillwyn. We were pretty much a wide spot in the road with a gas station on one end of the wide spot and a tasty freeze on the other."

"I get ya," I said, and I told him I was from Appalachiastan, so I knew. He asked me where the hell Appalachiastan was, and I told him my part of it was West "By God" Virginia, and he asked me why I called it Appalachiastan, because it made it sound like a third world country. I asked him if he'd ever been there, and he said no, and I told him that if he had, he'd understand. He said, "so you're saying it's like a third world country over there?" and I said, "In many ways, yes," and he said, "so it's fitting," and I said yes.

"So you'd see crazy 'ol Roy," he continued, "riding down to the gas station mostly to buy his beer every day. He only got gas once a month, cause that mower got real good fuel mileage, see. And you'd usually see him going to the gas station late morning, just after he woke up with a hangover. And you'd see him driving down to the Tasty Freeze just before sundown, no matter what time of year it was. If it was winter, he'd ride down there and get his dinner around four thirty, and if it was summer, he'd ride down there and get his dinner around eight thirty. Hell, I don't reckon the 'ol boy even had a watch or a clock in that mobile home of his he lived in back by the ballpark."

"Now wait a minute," I said to Michael, interrupting him. "You were saying earlier that this little wide spot in the road of yours only had a gas station and a Tasty Freeze. Now you're telling me it had a ballpark, too?"

"Oh, that's just what we called it," Michael said. "It really wasn't nothing but a wide spot off the side of the road of the wide spot along the road that made up our town. And it's where we kids would go play ball, or just sit around and hang out, so we just always called it the ballpark."

"I get it," I said, and I did, so it was most definitely fitting.

"So crazy 'ol Roy," Michael continued, "he had him a mobile home set up back behind the ballpark, just there at the edge of the woods."

"Uh, huh," I said, following.

"And most nights, and it didn't matter what time of year it was, he'd sit out there with his beer, I think he drank Stroh's. You ever heard of that?"

"Oh yea," I said. "Remember, I'm from Appalachiastan."

"That's right," Michael said. "So he'd sit out there with his Stroh's, and a flashlight, and a .22 caliber long rifle."

"What the hell would he do that for?" I asked.

"Well," Michael said. "He'd claim to be huntin' rabbits, up until around the time he got drunk. After that, he'd tell you he'd seen a Bigfoot Sasquatch up in the woods, back behind his mobile home, long time ago, like when he was a kid, and that he was gonna kill it and get rich and famous and leave our little wide spot alongside the road. Claimed he was gonna move to Charlottesville and buy him one of those fancy smancy houses close to the University and go to all the tennis matches."

"Was he a tennis fan?" I asked.

"Nah," Michael said. "He was just crazy. Thought maybe being seen at tennis matches might make him look more important."

"Oh," I said, and sat back to listen. Now, I was keeping my eye on our lines, because some of those big 'ol catfish were starting to swim their way past that long. The one where our baited hooks was only ten yards on the other side. I figured if the water temperatures dropped by another one or two degrees, those big 'ol fish might just be able to make it over there and take one of our baited hooks, without putting themselves out too much, due to the heat and all, and some of these fish had to weigh at least fifty pounds. You get down to the Richmond part of the James River, and you can catch catfish that way one hundred pounds all day long. I guess maybe they float down there from up here on these super hot summer days, and they're so danged big and heavy they just can't make it back up the river, so they end up just staying down there in Richmond.

"So me and this friend of mine," Michael was saying, "we were out here passing a football around one evening, and crazy 'ol Roy was over there with his .22, looking for rabbits or Bigfoot Sasquatch, or whatever. My friend, by the way, actually made it to Charlottesville, by way of a football scholarship to play for UVA. Made it to the NFL and won a superbowl. His name was Wendal Full. Ever heard of him?"

"Nope," I said.

"Anyways," Michael continued. "We just always figured he was just sitting outside drinking. And well, just about the time it was almost too dark to see, we heard that 'ol bladeless riding lawn mower's engine fire up and take off across the field. About ten second later we heard crazy 'ol Roy start a firing away with his .22."

"Was he trying to chase down a rabbit and shoot it while riding his bladeless riding lawn mower?" I asked.

"Well," Michael said. "That's what we thought. But we looked over, and crazy 'ol Roy was running behind the mower, about twenty yards back, shooting at the mower."

"What the hell?" I said. "Had he fallen off the mower, and he was shooting at his runaway mower?"

"That's what we thought," Michael said. "But when we took a good hard look at the mower, and mind you, it was right at the time of day when it was just almost too dark to see, but we squinted real hard, and by God, if we didn't see something big, and something dark, and something hairy riding away on that bladeless riding lawn mower."

"So you're telling me," I said, "that it appeared as if Bigfoot Sasquatch stole crazy 'ol Roy's bladeless riding lawn mower and then rode off on it?"

"That's exactly what I'm telling you," Michael said. "I ain't asking you to believe me, but that's how I remember it."

"Damn," I said. "I think you just cured my writer's block."

"How's that?" Michael asked.

"Well," I said. "This would make a great story for my next volume of the Bigfoot Sasquatch Files series I've been writing. Would you mind if I actually retold this story in a book?

"That'd be great," Michael said, and he smiled real big, lighting up like a Christmas tree. But after a hot minute, he said, "wait a minute."

"What's that?" I said.

"I'm not so sure that I want people knowing I told you this story."

"Why not?" I asked him.

"Well," he said. "If people heard me tell a story like this, they'd think I was as crazy as crazy 'ol Roy."

"Hm," I said, looking into the river in contemplation, and hoping those big 'ol fifty pound catfish would swim about another five yards over. "I've got it!" I said. "I'll change your name. I'll tell everyone your name was Michael."

"That'll work," he said. "For a start."

"What do you mean for a start?" I asked him.

"Well," he said. "I told you where I worked. What I retired from. If anyone down this way reads your story, they'll put two and two together, and they'll figure out who I am."

"Nah," I said. "I'll tell them you retired from the post office." I used to work for the post office, so it was the first thing to come to mind.

"That'll work," Michael said. Then we both sat in silence. He was looking for more holes we'd need to drill into the story, to protect his real identity, and I was hoping he wasn't going to back out of letting me use it, because it was a good one.

"What about my friend," Michael finally said. "I don't want to make it look like I'm one of those insecure name droppers by having named my buddy from childhood who went on to win a super bowl."

"I'll say his name is Wendell Full," I said. "No one will know who that is, because it's not a real person."

"Man," Michael said. "You *are* really good at this writing thing."

"Well," I said, feeling flattered. "I'm no Mark Twain, but I've put my time in. Been doing it for years."

Michael sat back for a minute, pondering a bit, and then he said, "you know, this place is so small, that I'm still afraid folks who read your story might figure out who told it to you, and they'd laugh me plum out of Buckingham County."

He had a point. People are pretty smart. They don't just believe what they read or see on the news. They question it. They think it might all be a bunch of highly spun half truths. And they know there might be more facts.

"I've got it!" I said. "In the story, I'll make you a black man!"

"Now you're talking," Micheal said. "And you know what? You should make crazy 'ol Roy white!"

"Done!" I said, "and I'll even say we were in Buckingham County, so even if anyone who might know you reads it, they'll never know it was you, because it didn't even happen in the place you lived your whole life!"

And just like that, we had ourselves an agreement on our story. Our little fishing tale, of sorts, and yes, that pun was intended.

Just about that time, one of those ginormous catfish *did* make its way over far enough on the other side of that log to take my baited hook. It hit so hard that it nearly pulled my rod into the river!

I jumped up and I started pulling and reeling. I didn't even need to set the hook, because that son of a gun had done it himself when he took the bait.

I reeled and reeled, but it was to to avail. This catfish was so big, he plum wore me out, and I had to actually hand the pole to Michael and let him reel for a while while I rested.

Once I got my wind and my strength back, I took the pole back from Michael, and it took me until well after dark to get that big 'ol catfish into the bank, but I by God did, and what a big one he was!

How big?

Well, he sure was a whopper!

I'd tell you.

But you wouldn't believe me.

The End!

If you enjoyed these stories, please consider reading all of the Bigfoot Sasquatch Files volumes, as well as all Kevin E Lake short story collections and novels, which are available on Amazon.

Also, if you enjoy stories told in the old fashion way, orally, please consider subscribing to Lake's YouTube channel, Homesteading Off The Grid.

As always, I, Kevin E Lake, the author, thank you for the time you took to read what I've written. We all know it's time you'll never EVER get back, and that *does* mean something to me.

I appreciate you.

See you next time.

No *potentially* about it!

Made in the USA
Middletown, DE
07 August 2020